Mouse

Squirrels

Snake

Whale

Brian Bat

To Alessandra, Christian, Tracey,
and Marcia—thanks for the help!

This book is set in Century 725/Monotype; Grilled Cheese BTN/Fontbros

Library of Congress Cataloging-in-Publication Data

Willems, Mo, author, illustrator.
  The thank you book / by Mo Willems.—First edition.
      pages cm
  "An Elephant & Piggie Book."
  Summary: "Piggie is determined to thank everyone she knows, but Gerald thinks she will forget someone important"—Provided by publisher.
  ISBN 978-1-4231-7828-6
  [1. Gratitude—Fiction. 2. Pigs—Fiction. 3. Elephants—Fiction. 4. Animals—Fiction. 5. Friendship—Fiction.] I. Title.
  PZ7.W65535Td 2016
  [E]—dc23   2015001585

Visit www.hyperionbooksforchildren.com and www.pigeonpresents.com

Printed in the United States of America
Reinforced binding

First Edition, May 2016
10 9
FAC-034274-20148

An ELEPHANT & PIGGIE Book

Hyperion Books for Children / New York

Squirrels!

Piggie!

Snake!

Piggie!

14

The Pigeon!

Thank you for
never giving up.

21

25

THANKS, WHALE!

You are nice!

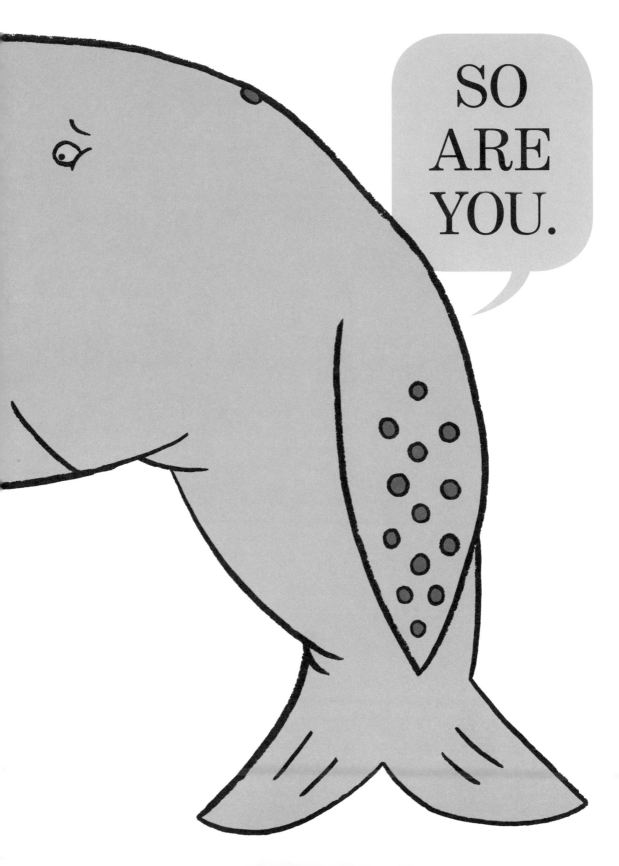

Ice Cream Penguin!

Thank you for your ice cream.

It is what
I do.

Doctor
Cat!

Piggie?

Brian Bat!

Piggie.

GIE!

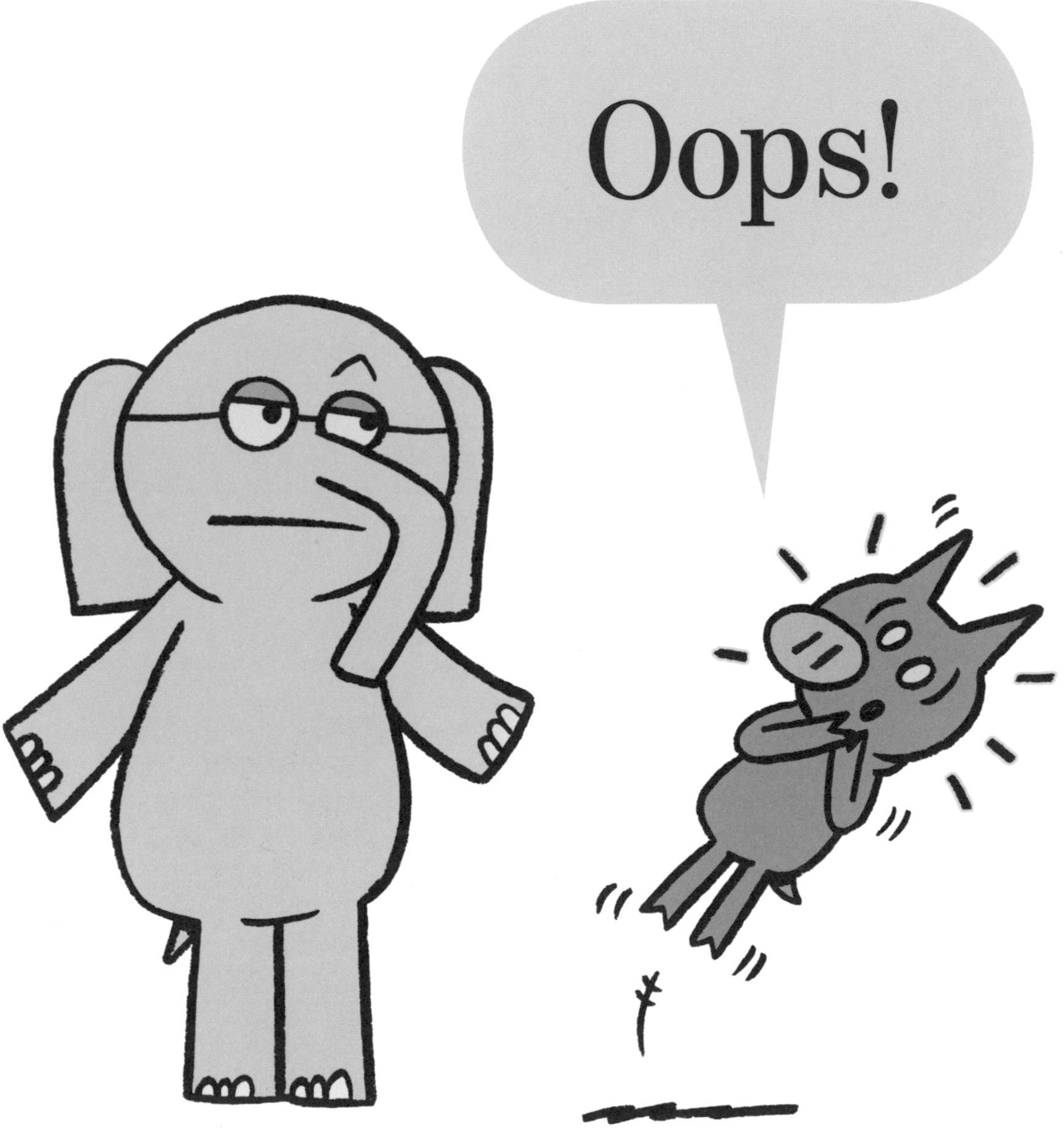
Oops!

That means a lot
to me, Piggie.

54

The Flies

Have you read all of Elephant and Piggie's funny adventures?

Elephant Gerald

Piggie